The White Cat and the Orange Bat

Who...who would do such a thing as this?

The apples are orange
And the oranges are blue!

The leaves are green
This part is true.

Oh my Oh my, How oh How could this happen?

The mailbox has blue dots
And the grass has orange spots.

The door has blue stripes
And the old man yells and gripes!

Soon it was easy to see, to see, to see.

There is a bat with paint
It makes me feel faint.

A bat with no hair
What a frightful scare.

Meow?

Oh no! Oh no! The bat sees the cat!

The cat's hair stands on end
As he starts to defend.

The bat comes near
The cat feels fear.

What to do, Oh what to do?

The cat sees a pipe
And runs through.

But the bat feels hype
And begins to pursue.

"My tail, My tail, It is so long."

The cat stops to breath
Pulling his tail through a wreathe.

The bat catches up with a quick hush
And readies his paint brush.

Brush brush brush, the paint flew all over.

"My tail is now orange"
"And my ears are blue!"

The bat sees this
He knows it is true.

Oh why, Oh why did this come to be?

The cat asks, "Why was this done to me?"
"How could this be the new me?"

The bat said, "I am orange, it is true."
"Now your ears are blue, blue, blue."

WOW!

And what of his tail? The cat started to hiss...

"I was happy all white"
Said the now colorful cat.

"But, you look so cool"
The bat said with a drool.

Hisss!
I am out of here !!

"What will I do, Oh what will I do?"

The cat thought of school
Would he look cool?

The bat gave a whirl and shout
"This is wonderful," as he flew about.

Nice!
Yay!

It is Great, Great, Great! This new found fate!

"I will rule, rule, rule,"
He thought he was cool.

So the bat flew away
And the cat danced back home.

ScHoOl is CoOl !

KinDneSs RocKs!

MaTh is My FrieNd !

The End

EnGlish is AweSoMe !

I LoVe my fRiEnDs !

NEVER be mean to others =)

www.ingramcontent.com/pod-product-compliance
Lightning Source LLC
LaVergne TN
LVHW071112160826
845679LV00004B/1053
9798366536400